The First Family of HOPE

The OBAMAS

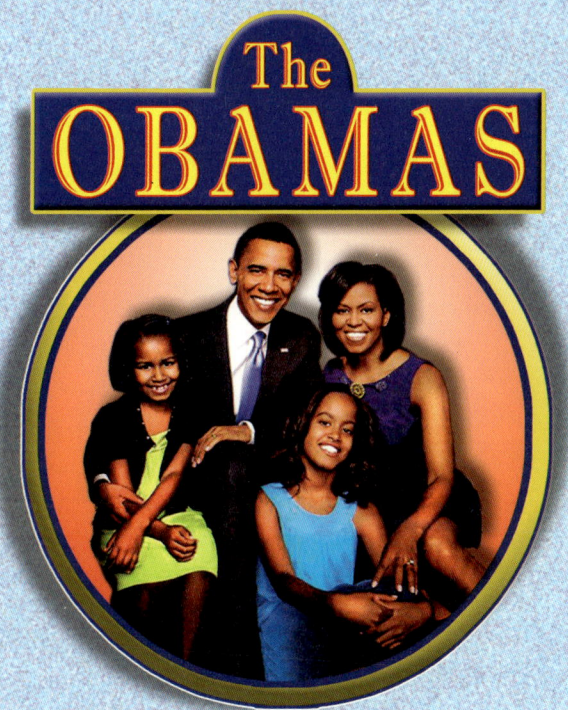

Barack

Michelle

Malia

Sasha

The Obama Family Tree

Obama Mania

Obama Mania

Hal Marcovitz

Mason Crest Publishers

Produced by 21st Century Publishing and Communications, Inc.

Copyright © 2009 by Mason Crest Publishers. All rights reserved. No part of this publication may be reproduced or transmitted in any form or by any means, electronic or mechanical, including photocopying, recording, taping, or any information storage and retrieval system, without permission from the publisher.

MASON CREST PUBLISHERS INC.
370 Reed Road
Broomall, Pennsylvania 19008
(866) MCP-BOOK (toll free)
www.masoncrest.com

Printed in the United States of America.

First Printing

9 8 7 6 5 4 3 2 1

Library of Congress Cataloging-in-Publication Data

Marcovitz, Hal.
　Obama mania / Hal Marcovitz.
　　p. cm. — (The Obamas)
　Includes bibliographical references and index.
　ISBN 978-1-4222-1482-4 (hardcover : alk. paper)
　ISBN 978-1-4222-1489-3 (pbk. : alk. paper)
　1. Obama, Barack—Juvenile literature. 2. Presidents—United States—Biography—Juvenile literature. 3. Racially mixed people—United States—Biography—Juvenile literature. I. Title.
E901.1.O23M37 2009
973.932092—dc22
[B]
　　　　　　　　　　　　　　　　　　　　　　　　　　　2009001903

Publisher's notes:
All quotations in this book come from original sources, and contain the spelling and grammatical inconsistencies of the original text.

The Web sites mentioned in this book were active at the time of publication. The publisher is not responsible for Web sites that have changed their addresses or discontinued operation since the date of publication. The publisher will review and update the Web site addresses each time the book is reprinted.

Contents

	Introduction	6
	Obama Family Timeline	8
1	The Country Catches Obama Fever	11
2	The Man Behind the Mania	17
3	The Obama Buzz Begins	25
4	Everything Obama	37
5	Obama Mania Continues	49
	Chronology	58
	Fun Facts	59
	Glossary	60
	Further Reading & Internet Resources	61
	Index	62
	Picture Credits	64
	About the Author	64

Introduction

On November 4, 2008, Barack Obama made history—he was the first black American to be elected president of the United States. The Obama family—Barack, wife Michelle, and daughters Malia and Sasha, became the first African-American first family.

THE FIRST FAMILY OF HOPE

The stories of the Obamas are fascinating and uniquely American. The six books in this series take you center stage and behind the scenes, with crafted and insightful storytelling, as well as hundreds of dynamic and telling photographs. Discover six unique inside perspectives on the Obama family's extraordinary journey and the Obama mania that surrounds it.

WHERE IT ALL BEGAN

Many generations ago, in the late 1600s, Barack's mother's ancestors arrived in colonial America as white emigrants from Europe, while his father's ancestors lived in villages in Kenya, Africa. Michelle's ancestors were shipped from Africa to America as slaves.

Generations later, Barack, son of a black father and a white mother, spent his childhood in Hawaii and Indonesia; while Michelle, a descendant of slaves, was growing up in Chicago. Later they both graduated from Harvard Law School, got married, and became proud parents of two beautiful daughters. Barack tackled injustice as a community organizer in Chicago, later entered politics, and was elected to the U.S. Senate.

"THE AUDACITY OF HOPE"

In 2004, at the Democratic National Convention, Barack Obama made an electrifying keynote speech, "The Audacity of Hope." He asked Americans to find unity in diversity and hope in the future. His message resonated with the attendees and millions of television viewers. Barack was catapulted from obscurity into the spotlight, and the Obama phenomenon had begun.

"YES WE CAN!"

On February 10, 2007, Barack announced his candidacy for the office of president of the United States. His family and legions of volunteers all over the country campaigned vigorously for him, and nearly two years later, the Obama family stood proudly in front of more than 240,000 supporters who gathered to hear Barack's victory speech. Tears streamed down the

The Obamas (left to right) Malia, Michelle, Sasha, and Barack, wave to their devoted fans. Barack has energized millions of people in the United States and around the world with his message of unity and hope.

faces of people who believed this was nothing short of a miracle. Tens of millions of television viewers worldwide watched and listened with a renewed sense of hope as President-elect Obama proclaimed:

> **"This victory is yours. . . . If there is anyone out there who still doubts that America is a place where all things are possible; who still wonders if the dream of our founders is alive in our time; who still questions the power of our democracy, tonight is your answer."**

OBAMA FAMILY TIMELINE

1600s to 1700s — Barack Obama's mother's ancestors immigrate to the American colonies from Europe.

1700s to 1800s — Michelle Robinson Obama's ancestors arrive in the American colonies as slaves.

1850s — Michelle's great-great grandfather is born a slave in South Carolina.

1936 — Barack Obama, Sr., Barack's father, is born in a small village in Kenya, Africa.

1937 — Michelle's mother, Marian Shields, is born.

1942 — Barack's mother, Ann Dunham, is born in Kansas.

1964 — Barack's parents, Barack Obama, Sr. and Ann Dunham are divorced.

1967 — Barack's mother marries Lolo Soetoro and moves the family to Soetoro's home country, Indonesia.

1971 — Barack returns to Hawaii and lives with his grandparents.

1600   1900   1950   1982

1912 — Michelle's grandfather, Fraser Robinson Jr., is born.

1918 — Barack's grandfather, Stanley Dunham, is born.

1922 — Barack's grandmother, Madelyn Payne, is born.

1935 — Michelle's father, Fraser Robinson III, is born.

1959 — Barack Obama, Sr. comes to America as a student.

February 21, 1961 — Barack Obama, Sr. and Ann Dunham are married.

August 4, 1961 — Barack is born in Honolulu, Hawaii.

January 17, 1964 — Michelle is born in Chicago, Illinois.

1979 — Barack graduates from high school and enrolls in Occidental College in Los Angeles, California.

1981 — Barack transfers to Columbia University in New York City.

1982 — Barack's father dies in Kenya, Africa.

Timeline (top, above axis)

1988 — Michelle graduates from Harvard Law School.

1988 — Barack enters Harvard Law School.

1990 — Barack is elected president of the *Harvard Law Review*.

1991 — Barack graduates from Harvard Law School.

1995 — Barack's first book, *Dreams from My Father*, is published.

1998 — Barack and Michelle's first daughter, Malia, is born.

2001 — Barack and Michelle's second daughter, Sasha, is born.

July 2004 — Barack delivers keynote speech at Democratic National Convention.

November 2, 2008 — Barack's grandmother dies in Hawaii.

November 4, 2008 — Barack is elected the first African-American president of the United States.

January 20, 2009 — Barack is sworn in as the 44th president of the United States.

Timeline axis: 1983 — 1995 — 2006 — 2009

Timeline (bottom, below axis)

1983 — Barack graduates from Columbia University.

1985 — Michelle graduates from Princeton University.

1985 — Barack moves to Chicago, Illinois, to work as a community organizer.

1988 — Barack visits his relatives in Kenya, Africa.

1992 — Barack and Michelle are married.

1992 — Barack begins teaching at the University of Chicago Law School.

1995 — Barack's mother dies.

1996 — Barack is elected to the Illinois State Senate.

November 2004 — Barack is elected to the U.S. Senate.

2006 — Barack's second book, *The Audacity of Hope*, is published.

February 10, 2007 — Barack announces his candidacy for the office of president of the United States of America.

August 2008 — Barack is nominated as the Democratic candidate for the presidency.

Celebrations of Obama's victory nationwide (clockwise from top left): Grant Park, Chicago; Times Square, New York City; Berkeley, CA; and Milwaukee, WI. Anticipation had been building during Obama's campaign, especially among younger voters. The excitement reached a fever pitch after Obama's election on November 4, 2008.

① The Country Catches Obama Fever

For nearly two years, Barack Obama had been followed by huge, overflowing crowds that often waited hours to hear his message of delivering change and unity to a divided nation. On the night of November 4, 2008, the biggest crowd ever gathered in Chicago's Grant Park to hear Barack speak yet again, but this time as the nation's president-elect.

Barack was unlike other politicians people had seen over the years. An African American, his sweeping victory over Senator John McCain of Arizona was truly awesome, welcomed by millions of Americans as well as millions of people in other countries.

Never before had an African American been elected to the nation's highest office.

But there was more to his appeal than race. Barack is a dynamic speaker. Moreover, his modest upbringing resonated with people who always rooted for the little guy. And, finally, his message of unity struck a cord among voters whose political leaders always seemed to be dissing one another. Some months earlier, one of Barack's supporters, Congressman Elijah Cummings of Maryland, summed it all up when he introduced the Illinois senator and presidential candidate to a crowd in Baltimore. He said,

> "This is not a campaign for president of the United States. This is a movement to change the world."

Compared to Kennedy

Barack's appeal has often been compared to that of John F. Kennedy, the 35th president who served from January 1961 until his assassination in November 1963. Both young senators emerged as dynamic spokesmen for new generations of Americans anxious to shoulder the responsibility of leadership. Kennedy said in his inaugural address,

> "Ask not what your country can do for you. Ask what you can do for your country."

Barack's message has often been similar. During his campaign for the presidency, Barack repeated this statement many times: "We will invest in you. You invest in your country."

Among the many people who accepted that message were members of the Kennedy family, who became enthusiastic supporters of the Illinois senator. The late president's brother, Senator Edward M. Kennedy of Massachusetts, enthusiastically endorsed Barack. Other members of the family who backed Barack were Caroline Kennedy, the late president's daughter, and Maria Shriver, Caroline's cousin and wife of California Governor Arnold Schwarzenegger. Caroline Kennedy endorsed Barack in a column published in the *New York Times* headlined, "A President Like My Father."

The Country Catches Obama Fever

Iowa students wait in line to sign up to volunteer in Obama's campaign. Young voters were drawn to Obama not only because he was different from other candidates who were Washington "insiders" but also because of his message of unity, change, and hope.

YOUNG VOLUNTEERS

Barack had announced his candidacy for the presidency 21 months earlier. At the time, he was well behind the front-runner, Senator Hillary Rodham Clinton of New York, who was much better known and a far bigger star on the national political scene. But Barack's campaign soon began to gain traction. His campaign managers made good use of the Internet, tapping deeply into the cyber community to spread the senator's message and raise campaign funds. By the time the election was over, Barack had raised more than $700 million, most of it through small donations made over the Internet by millions of followers.

OBAMA MANIA

A newspaper issue devoted to Obama's victory. In the last months of the campaign a frenzy of TV, magazine, and newspaper articles spread throughout the country, and the historic election of an African-American president created a flood of media coverage throughout the world.

The Country Catches Obama Fever

He also zoomed to the front of the field thanks in large part to the legions of young volunteers who flocked to his campaign offices. One of those volunteers was Ross Avila, a college student from Philadelphia who took time off from school to campaign in New Jersey, South Carolina, and Iowa. Indeed, Avila spent the winter of 2008 in Iowa, trudging from door to door in single-digit temperatures. He said,

> "Iowa in January was so miserable. I can't imagine doing such grueling work for someone that I didn't believe in so much."

CELEBRATION IN GRANT PARK

At Grant Park, Barack strode onto the stage accompanied by his wife, Michelle, and daughters Malia and Sasha. It was just an hour after the network TV **anchors** declared him the winner over McCain. In the audience, the cameras caught TV talk show host Oprah Winfrey and **civil rights** leader Jesse Jackson weeping as Barack prepared to speak. Addressing some 240,000 people in the crowd, as well as more than 70 million watching on TV, Barack said,

> "What began twenty-one months ago in the depths of winter must not end on this autumn night. This victory alone is not the change we seek—it is only the chance for us to make that change. And that cannot happen if we go back to the way things were. It cannot happen without you.
>
> So let us summon a new spirit of patriotism; of service and responsibility where each of us resolves to pitch in and work harder and look after not only ourselves, but each other."

Barack poses for a photo after being elected the first African-American president of the *Harvard Law Review*. This election began a series of firsts for Obama, each one gathering more attention in the press. His background, abilities, and focus on helping others made great stories for journalists and publishers.

②

The Man Behind the Mania

Barack burst into national headlines long before he harbored ambitions to run for president. In 1990, while attending Harvard University Law School, Barack won election as the first African-American president of the *Harvard Law Review*, the prestigious publication that comments on important court cases in America. Newspapers soon sent reporters to the Harvard campus to report on the history-making election.

Journalists soon published stories on the unusual background of the new *Law Review* president—his ethnicity as the son of a white mother and black father, a childhood spent mostly in Indonesia, and a decision to give up a high-paying corporate job to spend five years as a community organizer. In interviewing Barack and others, the journalists uncovered a story of an immensely popular individual who hoped his election would open new doors for African Americans in the legal community. Wrote the *Boston Globe*,

> **It is entirely characteristic of Obama, a man of substantial accomplishments, that he would view his success in terms of American blacks and minorities in general rather than a personal victory.**

The *Globe* also sought out people who knew Barack when he had worked as a community organizer in Chicago. One of his former co-workers, John Owens, said that Barack was dedicated to helping individuals find better housing and employment opportunities, but he also felt he could help change the system that had long been stacked against poor people. Said Owens,

> **I thought, 'This guy sounds like he's president of the country already.' I've never met anyone who could leave that impression after only five minutes.**

Commentary on Race Relations

Such stories captured the eyes of editors at a New York publisher, who offered Barack a contract to write a book, soon to be titled *Dreams from My Father*. The book was in some respects an **autobiography**, relating Barack's early years growing up in Hawaii and Indonesia and his 1988 trip back to Kenya to explore his roots and discover the truth about his father, a man he barely knew. *Dreams from My Father* was also a commentary on race relations in America, making the case that if a young biracial man from Hawaii can accept the fact that he is a part of two races, Americans may be willing to accept a multiracial society as well. Barack told an interviewer,

The Man Behind the Mania

A man at a rally holds a copy of Barack's book, *Dreams from My Father*, which became a best seller. One undecided voter wrote in 2007, "I'm leaning toward Obama. . . . But regardless of what sort of president he would make, . . . anyone who could write this book must be a pretty amazing person."

❝ America is getting more complex. The color line in America being black and white is out the window. That does break down barriers. People can come together around values and not just race. ❞

Critics praised the book. *Crisis* magazine wrote,

❝ His efforts to bring the tools of self-discovery and empowerment to those who need them most are very much an extension of the personal journey recounted in *Dreams from My Father*. . . . In a world where tribal

OBAMA MANIA

loyalties—black, white, American, African, European—often collide, Obama's story is a journey that speaks to all races, to all peoples."

A MULTICULTURAL BACKGROUND

Barack visited Kenya shortly before enrolling in law school. Twenty-seven years before, in 1961, he had been born in Hawaii, the son of a mixed race couple. His mother, Stanley Ann Dunham, grew up in Kansas and suburban Seattle, Washington; his father, Barack Hussein Obama Sr., was a Kenyan who won a **scholarship** to study at the University of Hawaii and later Harvard University. The two divorced after only three years of marriage; Barack was just two years old.

Barack with his mother, Stanley Ann (left); and with his father, Barack Obama Sr. in 1971 (right). As a biracial child Barack had a difficult journey of self discovery. Later, his books helped readers break down stereotypes, look beyond race, and talk about important issues that could help unify America.

The Bench Jockey

While living in Hawaii Barack made his high school basketball team, which won a state championship in 1979. Barack was not a starter, but he perfected a good hook shot and whenever he came off the bench his hustle and desire to score impressed others, earning him the nickname "Barry O'Bomber."

He was also something of a team spokesman, particularly for the bench jockeys. During games it was not unusual for Barack to confront the coach and demand more playing time. Said Suzanne Maurer, the mother of Darren Maurer, one of Barack's teammates,

"I recall that he was the type that if he had a dream, he would pursue it. The sky seemed to be the limit, and Barry was very much a can-do person, even with sports, even as a benchwarmer."

Stanley Ann married again and the family moved to Indonesia. In 1971, she sent Barack and his half-sister Maya back to Hawaii to be raised by her parents. After high school, Barack enrolled in Occidental College in Los Angeles and later transferred to Columbia University in New York, where he earned a degree.

After spending five years as a community organizer, he enrolled at Harvard. While working as a summer **intern** for a prestigious Chicago law firm, he was **mentored** by another Harvard graduate, Michelle Robinson. A romance soon developed, and in 1992 Michelle and Barack married. In 1998, the couple's first daughter, Malia, was born; she was followed in 2001 by a younger sister, Sasha.

POLITICAL AMBITIONS WITH A MOVIE-STAR SMILE

By 1995, the Obamas had been living in Chicago for three years when Barack won his first election, a campaign for the state Senate. He went on to win re-election twice, but his political career stumbled when he entered a **primary** for a U.S. House seat and was easily defeated. Barack learned an important lesson from the race—that he had failed to deliver a meaningful message to the voters, and that the sole reason he entered the race was to advance his own career.

He spent the next four years working in the Democratic trenches, doing favors for other political candidates, working hard on legislation in the Illinois state capital of Springfield, and making alliances with powerful forces in the Illinois Democratic Party. In 2003, when it appeared a U.S. Senate seat would open the following year, Barack put out feelers to Democratic leaders on whether they would support him for the slot. Their responses were surprisingly enthusiastic.

An Eye on the White House

Michelle's brother, Craig Robinson, found himself immediately impressed with Barack. As the two got to know one another, they played basketball together and although far less talented than Robinson, Barack soon impressed his future brother-in-law with his game and will to win. (Craig attended Princeton University on a basketball scholarship and later played professionally in Europe before returning to the United States to coach college basketball.) When Michelle started dating Barack, Craig decided to judge his sister's new boyfriend on the court, so he often played against Barack one-on-one. It was during this time that Barack confided to Robinson that he saw himself being elected to the presidency.

Recalled Craig, "Barack was like, 'Well, I wanna be a politician. You know, maybe I can be president of the United States.' And I said, 'Yeah, yeah, okay, come over and meet my Aunt Gracie—and don't tell anybody that!'"

It was during the 2004 race for the U.S. Senate that Barack hit his stride. He proved himself to be a dynamic speaker whose words could captivate large audiences. Voters were enthralled with his personal story as well as his call for a change in Washington's divisive brand of politics. In early 2004, as Barack's campaign was getting off the ground, the *Chicago Sun-Times* published a

The Man Behind the Mania

Barack flashes a smile and shakes hands with kids who are still too young to vote during his 1995 campaign for the Illinois State Senate. Even in early campaigns, Obama captured the media's attention and voters' imaginations. These kids would be old enough to cast their votes in 2008.

list of political figures the newspaper believed were poised to capture the public's imagination. Barack's name headed the list. The newspaper wrote,

> **"The first African-American president of the *Harvard Law Review* has a movie-star smile and more than a little mystique.... Also, we just like to say his name."**

Delegates cheer as Barack Obama delivers the keynote speech at the 2004 Democratic National Convention in Boston. His dramatic speech thrust Obama into the national spotlight and began the media buzz that fueled constant speculation on his future in politics.

3

The Obama Buzz Begins

On a broiling hot summer night in 2004, Barack took the stage at the Democratic National Convention in Boston to deliver the **keynote address**. His emotional 17-minute speech, titled "The Audacity of Hope," called for Americans to unite to solve the country's many problems. The speech is regarded as one of the political highlights of the 21st century.

Thousands of Democrats sat transfixed in their seats as Barack made his dramatic appeal for change. Watching the speech at home, millions of viewers felt themselves drawn in by the power of his oratory. He said,

OBAMA MANIA

> **"Tonight, we gather to affirm the greatness of our nation not because of the height of our skyscrapers, or the power of our military, or the size of our economy; our pride is based on a very simple premise, summed up in a declaration made over two hundred years ago: 'We hold these truths to be self-evident, that all men are created equal.'"**

People young and old were stoked by his words. Sixteen-year-old Theresa Becchi from Stamford, Connecticut, said,

Barack is surrounded by students during his appearance at Arizona State University in November 2005. People of all ages were energized and excited by Obama's 2004 keynote address, even though most had never heard of him before. After that speech he became a nationally known star politician.

The Obama Buzz Begins

> **"It was so amazing. . . . He's just kind of a new wave of the Democratic Party and I think he's going to do great and wonderful things if he succeeds in politics because he's such an amazing speaker."**

Joseph Lowery, president of the Southern Christian Leadership Conference, a civil rights group, said,

> **"I like what I see in Obama. I like his intellectual energy. He has given every signal that he is capable and has the mettle to continue the struggle."**

When 70-year-old convention volunteer Ruth Werksman encountered Barack in front of his hotel, she kissed him, asked for his autograph, and declared,

> **"You were fabulous. You spoke not as a black American, but as an American. That's what this nation is all about."**

And Oregonian Karol Collymore wrote on her **blog**,

> **"This striking man walked across the screen and my ears perked up. . . . I was completely mesmerized by this man called Barack Obama. His speech grabbed my heart and tears were running down my face."**

"Don't Screw It Up, Buddy."

It was Michelle who realized that Barack could emerge from the 2004 Democratic National Convention as a major national political figure. In the days leading up to his delivery of the keynote address, Michelle worked closely with her husband on the speech. Seconds before he walked onto the stage to deliver the speech, Michelle told him, "Just don't screw it up, buddy."

The following morning, Barack's picture appeared on the front pages of hundreds of newspapers, not only in America but across the globe. When CNN anchorman Bill Hemmer opened his network's convention coverage the morning after the speech, he said, "The Obama buzz is big today."

Themes of Change and Unity

Barack went on to win the 2004 Senate election. In 2006, his second book, *The Audacity of Hope*, was published. The book expands on the themes of change and unity he raised during his convention speech. Clearly, the book served as his declaration of how politics should be played in America. He wrote,

> "Not only [have] my encounters with voters confirmed the fundamental decency of the American people, they also reminded me that at the core of the American experience are a set of ideals that continue to stir our collective conscience; a common set of values that bind us together despite our differences; a running thread of hope that makes our improbable experiment in democracy work."

Like a Rock Star

In the meantime, the Obama phenomena that had started at the 2004 Democratic National Convention continued to spread throughout the country. By 2006, Barack had become the most requested speaker on the national campaign trail, appearing with Democratic candidates in more than 30 states. An article in *The Christian Science Monitor* entitled "What's driving Obamamania?" described one such event:

> "With standing room crowds chanting for the star to show, Sunday's Democratic fundraiser could have been a rock concert. . . . 'Right now, he's a rock star.' says Jim Craig, former Democratic leader in the New Hampshire House."

The Obama Buzz Begins

When asked if he intended to run for president, Barack said,

❝ This is an office you can't run for just on the basis of ambition. You have to feel deep in your gut that you have a vision for the country that is sufficiently important that it needs to be out there. ❞

It seemed Barack already had a clear vision for the country; On February 10, 2007, he announced his intentions to seek the presidency in 2008.

A large crowd gathers listens to Barack Obama speak during a rally in Iowa City, Iowa, November 2006. Barack had become the most requested speaker on the campaign trail, with crowds chanting for him as they would at a rock concert. And he hadn't even declared his presidential candidacy yet!

Young Voters the Key

Barack realized early in the campaign that young voters held the key to the election. In the past, young voters had proved to be unreliable—it was hard to get them to register to vote, hard to keep their interest, and hardest of all to get them to show up at the polls on election day.

Still, in Barack, young voters saw a different type of politician. Young people were overwhelmingly opposed to the Iraq War, and Barack had made his position on the war clear—if elected, he would order a withdrawal of American troops. Moreover, in Washington, it appeared to many young people that the politicians never accomplished much—the place was stuck in eternal gridlock. On TV, Washington politicians were always dissing one another. When young voters heard Barack speak, though, they heard a different message—one calling for politicians to resolve their differences and find a way to solve the nation's problems.

College students soon gave up their breaks to work for him in the early primary and **caucus** states. Some of the students took semesters off to knock on doors, register voters, and work

Barack's Speechmaking Skills

Barack's skill as a speechmaker is widely recognized and often regarded as a main reason voters flocked to support him in 2008. Some of that attraction was no doubt due to the professionalism of his speechwriters, who provided engaging and colorful words for him to speak. Experts believe, though, that Barack's natural gift for dramatic speechmaking won over many supporters.

Ted Widmer, a speechwriter for former President Bill Clinton, says,

"He is blessed with a richly resonant voice that we love to hear. He could read the telephone directory and it would sound good. He is very good at pauses and inflection, and he cuts an impressive figure on stage—all of which adds up to making an Obama speech a special event."

The Obama Buzz Begins

Student volunteers at the Obama campaign office in downtown San Francisco make phone calls to potential voters, 2008. Many college students took time off from school to work long hours registering voters and making phone calls in support of Obama. These students formed the core of Obama's volunteer army.

the phones for the young senator. "I think he's really going to do good things as president," said 18-year-old Syracuse University freshman Kim Ndobe, who campaigned for Obama in New Hampshire. "Like the war. I think we'd end that pretty soon, which would be great. My brother fought in Iraq, and it was really a stressful time. I don't want to go through that any more."

By the time the early primaries and caucuses rolled around in 2008, Barack had an effective field army of hundreds of volunteers on the ground.

Campaigning on the Internet

Barack and his advisors also knew that the key to keeping the attention of young voters could be found on the Internet. Barack's supporters started pushing his candidacy and his message on social networking sites and through e-mails. Hundreds of blogs were devoted to the campaign. Meanwhile, thousands of supporters uploaded images on the photo-sharing Web site Flickr, displaying cakes they baked to resemble the candidate, murals they painted of Barack on the sides of outdoor walls, and even tattoos that are now permanent parts of their bodies.

Soon, one of the most popular celebrities on the Internet was "Obama Girl," in reality a singer named Amber Lee Ettinger who sang about her devotion to Barack in a web-based video that was viewed millions of times on YouTube and similar sites.

"Obama in 30 Seconds"

The political advocacy group Moveon.org sponsored an "Obama in 30 Seconds" contest, inviting people to produce their own TV commercials supporting the candidate. More than 1,100 amateur filmmakers entered; their videos were posted on the group's Web site and viewed by some 5 million people. Hollywood actors Ben Affleck and Matt Damon served as judges for the competition.

The Moveon.org contest was an organized effort to promote Barack, but many people weren't interested in winning prizes for their pro-Barack videos, they simply wanted to post them where others could see them. By August 2008, more than 1,000 videos connected to Barack were posted on YouTube. Barack's MySpace page included nearly 500,000 friends. The only MySpace page with more friends belonged to teenage singer Miley Cyrus.

Setting Fundraising Records

Barack's campaign advisors also found the Internet could be an effective fund-raising tool. Making his appeals for campaign funds mostly on his Web site, Barack raised tens of millions of dollars a month. By the time the campaign ended a year later, he had raised

The Obama Buzz Begins

some $700 million, a record for an American political campaign. More than 3 million Americans contributed to the campaign, most making donations of less than $100.

HOPE AND PROGRESS

As the 2008 campaign began in earnest, Barack seemed to be everywhere—shooting baskets on TV, dancing on *The Ellen DeGeneris Show*, appearing on *Late Show with David Letterman* and *Saturday Night Live*. When hip-hop star will.i.am of the Black

Rapper will.i.am (in black) and singer/songwriter John Legend (in white) perform during the 2008 Democratic National Convention. Inspired by Obama's words, will.i.am wrote the campaign theme song "Yes We Can," which captured the nation's imagination. The rapper said, "When inspiration calls, you don't send it to voicemail; you answer it."

OBAMA MANIA

Eyed Peas wrote Barack's campaign theme song, "Yes We Can," it was downloaded onto millions of MP3 players—each download raising money for the campaign. Meanwhile, some of the biggest stars volunteered to perform the song in a campaign video, including actresses Scarlett Johansson, Kate Walsh, Kelly Hu, and

An Obama supporter holds up a "Hope" poster during a rally. Shepard Fairey's design became the iconic image of the Obama campaign, appearing on everything from T-shirts to the cover of *Time* magazine. The original stenciled portrait is now displayed at the Smithsonian's National Portrait Gallery.

Amber Valetta, singers John Legend and Nick Cannon, and actor John Rodriguez. On YouTube alone, the video was viewed some 15 million times.

The Fist Bump

As the final primary states cast their ballots, Barack made a major speech in St. Paul, Minnesota. After his introduction by Michelle, the candidate and his wife bumped fists. It was a touching and emotional gesture, but the world suddenly wanted to know what it meant. On Fox News, conservative commentator E.D. Hill suggested it might be a "terrorist fist jab."

Later, Michelle appeared on the TV show *The View*, and as she was introduced she declared, "I have to be greeted properly. Fist bump, please." She then exchanged fist bumps with the panelists, including Barbara Walters, Whoopi Goldberg, Joy Behar, Sherri Shepherd, and Elisabeth Hasselbeck. "But let me tell you, I'm not that hip," Michelle added. "I got this from the young staff. That's the new high-five."

When Los Angeles–based artist Shepard Fairey designed a funky and incandescent poster for Barack, giving the campaign a sense of urban cool, the campaign printing presses couldn't keep up with demand. The poster, in vivid blues and reds, depicts Barack wearing a look of firm resolve on his face. Beneath the image is the word "Hope," although Fairey also produced a later version depicting the word "Progress." Said the artist,

> "I wanted strong. I wanted wise, but not intimidating. . . . I wanted the poster . . . to be appealing to a younger, apathetic audience, yet tame enough not to be seen as radical or offensive to the more mainstream political participants. You want to create the most flattering shapes. Strong in the face of adversity."

Clockwise from top left: A little girl with an Obama poster; an Obama cookie; a bearded Obama supporter covered with buttons; and a coffee latte with Obama's face, in Germany, prior to the U.S. election. As Obama mania spread, the candidate's image appeared on merchandise and Internet Web sites throughout the world.

4

Everything Obama

As Barack took the stage in Berlin, Germany, in July of 2008, he looked over a sea of people that stretched far down the Tiergarten, the sprawling park in the center of the city. Later, newspapers would estimate that some 200,000 people crowded into the Tiergarten to hear the words of the candidate who had just wrapped up the Democratic nomination for president.

AN INTERNATIONAL TOUR

Just weeks before, Barack finally defeated Senator Clinton for the nomination. Throughout the campaign, he had been criticized for his lack of **foreign policy** experience, so once he nailed the nomination he made plans for an international tour.

First stop on the tour was the **Middle East**, where he met with political leaders and toured the war zones. In Kuwait, a country that borders Iraq, he found time to get in some basketball at a military base, stunning everyone in the crowd by hitting a shot from three-point range. Watching the event unfold, *Washington Post* **columnist** David Broder wrote,

> ❝ When, on the first day of the trip, Obama stepped onto a basketball court at the air base in Kuwait and sent his first three-point shot cleanly through the basket, you knew the gods had decided to favor him. ❞

After visiting the Middle East, Barack made plans to meet political leaders in France, Germany, and Great Britain. His stopover in Germany included an important speech to German citizens, promising them that America would seek to rebuild its standing among other countries. During the administration of President George W. Bush, the United States had done little to foster better relations with its allies as well as its enemies.

Beginning his speech, Barack extended his call for unity that had resonated so well among voters in the United States. Only by working together, Barack said, can nations solve the tremendous problems facing the world. He said,

> ❝ No one nation, no matter how large or powerful, can defeat such challenges alone. None of us can deny these threats, or escape responsibility in meeting them. . . .
>
> I know my country has not perfected itself. We've made our share of mistakes, and there are times when our actions around the world have not lived up to our best intentions. But I also know how much I love America. ❞

Everything Obama

More than 200,000 people gather in Berlin to hear Obama speak, July 24, 2008. The crowd cheered wildly and waved American flags. A family wearing "Vote Obama" T-shirts commented, "The United States' reputation has suffered greatly through Bush. That could change dramatically with Obama, and we hope it will."

OBAMA MANIA AROUND THE WORLD

As Barack spoke, Germans and others in the crowd waved tiny American flags—a rare gesture, because whenever Bush had visited foreign countries during his presidency demonstrators had often showed up to protest. Others in the Tiergarten crowd wore T-shirts or held signs that proclaimed Barack's campaign slogan, "Yes We Can."

Clearly, crowd members were stoked by Barack's words. Manfred Krause, 65, said Barack reminded him of the Reverend Martin Luther King Jr., the American civil rights leader who visited Berlin in 1964. As a young student, Krause attended King's

OBAMA MANIA

Clockwise from top left: an Obama statue and posters in a storefront in Obama City, Japan; hand-lettered Obama posters on the wall of a London pub; an Indian man who painted his face in support of Obama; and a Thailand for Obama T-shirt. After Barack's visits to the Middle East and Europe, his appeal spread throughout the world.

speech and found himself inspired by King's words. After hearing Barack, Krause said, "I thought, here is someone coming from the same place." Another member of the crowd, Gerda Schulz, said,

> **"I expect Obama to be a president who makes it possible to be proud of being a fan of the USA. In the last seven years [of the Bush administration], it was rather embarrassing here to say, 'I like Americans and I am thankful for what they did for us.'"**

The foreign media proclaimed the trip a success. "It seems that there are no other news stories in Germany other than the Obama visit," declared Cordula Meyer, a correspondent for the German magazine *Der Speigel*. "Europeans have fallen in love with the Democrat." Wrote the *International Herald-Tribune*, an English-language newspaper published in Paris, France:

> **"The excitement in Germany over Obama has grown steadily through the Democratic primaries, reaching its peak with his address here Thursday in the Tiergarten, in Berlin. . . . The crowd was filled with many American citizens. . . . But the overwhelming share was made up of German residents, who cheered when Obama called upon the United States to correct its deeds."**

A Social Movement

Clearly, the senator's appeal was now international—polls taken in Europe showed that 78 percent of French citizens and 72 percent of Germans said they would prefer to see Barack win the presidential election over John McCain. But in America, the polls remained close with Barack holding a lead of just a handful of points over McCain.

Still, when Barack returned from his international trip he found fervor for his candidacy growing. While Barack took the stump, focusing on such issues as his opposition to the war in Iraq and his plans to aid the faltering American economy, some of his most dedicated supporters instead concentrated on making his campaign into a social movement.

Craftspeople designed and sold jewelry in his likeness. Artists painted portraits of him. Animators featured him in their films. Bakers made cakes dedicated to him. Even knitters crocheted his face into blankets. Of course, everybody who created a piece of "Obama art" was anxious to show it off, and so they posted images of their handiwork on the Internet. One devoted fan posted an image of a Valentine's Day card featuring the candidate's image and the caption, "I want to Barack your world."

Barack O'Lanterns

As Halloween approached, many people carved Barack's image into pumpkins. The political news Web site Huffington Post published pictures of some of the best efforts, dubbing them "Barack O'Lanterns." In Pennsylvania, a farmer plowed over a field and painted a huge replica of Shepard Fairey's Hope poster on his land.

All the hoopla surrounding Barack was certainly gaining notice—even by supporters of McCain, who found themselves giving grudging props to the Illinois senator. Andrew Stuttaford, a columnist for the conservative *National Review*, said,

> **"The Obama campaign is, quite clearly, aimed more at the heart than the head. That may not please the more intellectually honest of his supporters, but, judging by the ecstatic response the senator has succeeded in generating among an impressive number of voters, it has been a very, very smart thing to do."**

Celebrity Endorsements

People who baked cakes, knitted blankets, and carved pumpkins were not the only enthusiastic backers of Barack's campaign. Early in 2008, many celebrities started endorsing Barack and contributing

Everything Obama 43

Zilly Rosen of ZillyCakes in Buffalo, New York, builds a likeness of Barack Obama using 1,240 cupcakes. Obama art was everywhere, ranging from cookies and cakes to jewelry, blankets, paintings, and even carved pumpkins. To some, this atmosphere was more like a social movement than a political campaign.

their time and money to his campaign. Oprah Winfrey was one of the first celebrities to endorse Barack. The TV talk show host with a large and loyal following announced her support for the senator on her show, then helped Barack raise $3 million by hosting a fund-raising event on the campus of the University of California-Los Angeles (UCLA) the morning of the 2008 Super Bowl. At the event, attended by some 9,000 fans, Winfrey told the guests,

OBAMA MANIA

> **"I believe that change has already come, California. I believe that change has already come because I know that you all just heard about this this morning and said, 'Let me get over there to UCLA' here on Super Bowl Sunday. We're all energized, we're excited and we're fired up."**

Other celebrities helped out as well. Actress Alfre Woodward and actor Ed Norton recorded telephone messages that were phoned to voters in key states. Actress Jennifer Aniston donated $2,300 to Barack's campaign while comedian Chris Rock and

Barack, his wife Michelle (right), and Oprah Winfrey wave to the crowd at a rally in Manchester, N.H., December 9, 2007. As the campaign progressed, more and more celebrities appeared at rallies and added their support, fund-raising skills, and donations to Obama's cause.

Everything Obama

his wife donated $4,600. Scarlett Johansson appeared at a rally in Iowa for Barack. Academy Award–winning actor Robert DeNiro appeared at a fund-raiser for Barack in New Jersey. Another Academy Award winner, Tom Hanks, posted his reasons for supporting Barack on his MySpace page.

The Biden Text

During the summer of 2008, as anticipation built over whom Barack would select as his running mate, the Obama campaign invited supporters to sign up for a text message on their cell phones that would alert them the moment Barack made his pick. At just after 3 A.M. on August 23, 2008, some 2.9 million text messages went out to supporters, announcing the selection of U.S. Senator Joe Biden of Delaware as Barack's choice for vice president.

The brief message read, "Barack has chosen Senator Joe Biden to be our VP nominee. Watch the first Obama-Biden rally live at 3 P.M. ET on www.BarackObama.com. Spread the word!"

It is believed to have been the single largest transmission of a simultaneous message in the history of cell phone texting. The message cost the campaign $290,000 because the cell phone company charged 10 cents for each message.

Meanwhile, actor Samuel L. Jackson skipped the Oscars to campaign for Barack in Texas. "We need somebody the world relates to in a very real kind of way," Jackson said. Actress Halle Berry told a reporter, "I'll do whatever [Barack] says to do. I'll collect paper cups off the ground to make his pathway clear." And actor George Clooney said, "He walks into a room and you want to follow him somewhere, anywhere."

COLLECTING A PIECE OF HISTORY

Others had their own interests in hyping Barack's candidacy—they hoped to score some cash off the Obama mania that was sweeping

OBAMA MANIA

Clockwise from top left: an Obama commemorative plate; stacks of Obama T-shirts; an Obama bag with the message "our time will come"; and high-heeled Obama shoes at a craft fair. Many merchandisers tried to make a profit from Obama's popularity by selling anything with his image on it; others donated a portion of their sales to Obama's campaign.

across the country. Some car dealers enlisted an actor—a dead-on Barack look-alike—to appear in TV commercials selling the Kia Sportage automobile. In the TV spot, the actor appeared before a raucous crowd, declaring, "Yes, you can!" The slight variation on Barack's campaign slogan was meant to fire up the car-buying public rather than promise a new sense of unity for Americans. Critics huffed that the commercial cheapened Barack's message, but there was no denying that the ad made people laugh.

On city streets, sidewalk vendors hawked all manner of Obama paraphernalia, such as coffee mugs, key chains, and refrigerator magnets. All the merchandise displayed images of Obama or his campaign slogan. Demand was so high that many vendors couldn't keep the merchandise in stock.

Other entrepreneurs turned to the Internet to do commerce in all things Obama. The online auction site eBay typically featured some 20,000 Obama items a day—among them campaign buttons, T-shirts, photographs, posters, cell phone covers, bobble-head dolls, and tote bags. Said A.J. Khubani, head of a company that manufactures dinner plates displaying Barack's image, "The climate's very hot. People want to collect a piece of history."

Barack on *SNL*

During the 2008 campaign, all the major candidates and other national figures found themselves appearing on *Saturday Night Live*—although not necessarily in person. The show's cast members often played the candidates, usually earning *SNL* big laughs as well as a big audience.

On the show, Barack was played by comic Fred Armisen while actor and comedian Will Ferrell made several appearances as President George W. Bush. But the impersonators who got the biggest laughs were comics Amy Poehler, who portrayed Hillary Clinton, and Tina Fey, who played John McCain's running mate, Governor Sarah Palin of Alaska. Clinton and Palin both made guest appearances on *SNL*, and while Clinton seemed to enjoy the gag, Palin is rumored to have been less than delighted with Fey's impersonation.

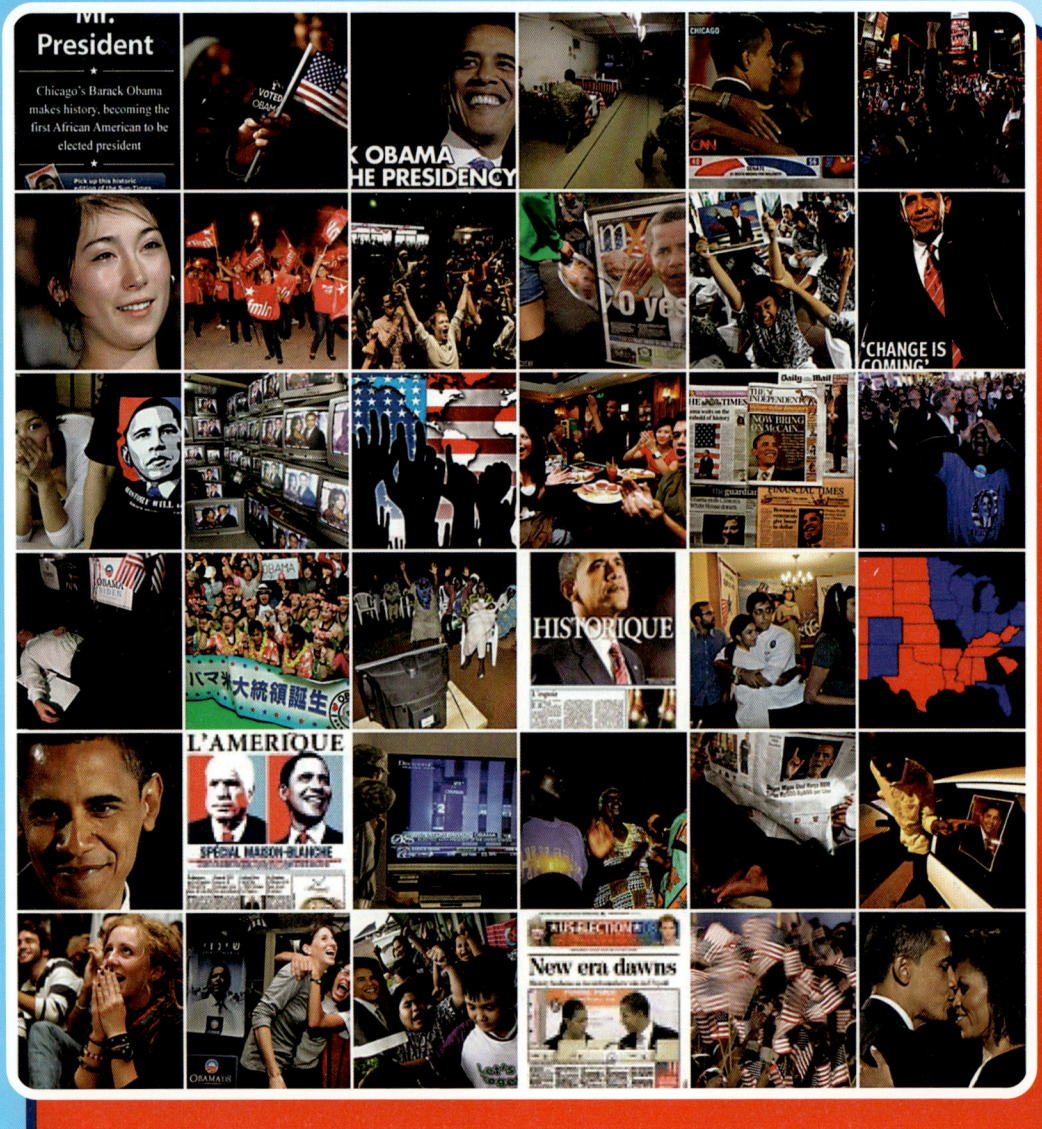

Photo collage of reactions around the world to Obama's victory. After the election, Obama mania continued, with congratulations pouring in from heads of state and even former candidates and opposition politicians. Everyone offered encouragement and a willingness to work with the new president.

5

Obama Mania Continues

As Barack took the stage in Grant Park as the nation's new president-elect, words of congratulations streamed in from all corners of the earth. World leaders transmitted their best wishes to Barack, indicating their willingness to work with the new president while acknowledging the historic nature of the election.

In Paris, President Nicholas Sarkozy said, "I give you my warmest congratulations and, through me, those of all French people. Your brilliant victory rewards a tireless commitment to serve the American people." In London, Prime Minister Gordon Brown said, "This is a moment that will live in history as long as history books are written." In Jerusalem, Israeli Foreign Minister spokesman Ygal Palmor said, "We are certain that Israel-American friendship faces a bright future." And in Pretoria, South African President Kgalema Motlanthe said, "Your election . . . carries with it hope for millions of your countrymen and women [and] for millions of people of . . . African descent."

From Rivals to Partners

Some of the warmest words were delivered by McCain who, after the grueling campaign, delivered a message of encouragement to the president-elect indicating, perhaps, that Barack's call for unity had resonated with the man who had been his most bitter adversary. Said McCain,

> **The American people have spoken, and they have spoken clearly. Senator Obama has achieved a great thing for himself and for his country. I applaud him for it. . . . These are difficult times for our country, and I pledge to him tonight to do all in my power to help him lead us through the many challenges we face.**

McCain wasn't the only former rival to offer congratulations to the president-elect. Senator Clinton called Barack just moments after he left the Grant Park stage. She said,

> **Tonight, we are celebrating an historic victory for the American people. This was a long and hard fought campaign but the result was well worth the wait.**

In the weeks following the election, Barack and Clinton would find themselves in agreement on many issues. In fact, Barack selected Clinton as his secretary of state. An important position in the **cabinet**, the secretary of state is charged with representing the president in negotiations with foreign heads of state. Clinton would go on to play a pivotal role in Barack's plans to bring the troops home from Iraq.

Obama Mania Continues

Barack Obama and Senator Hillary Clinton at a 2008 campaign event in Unity, N.H. As president-elect, Barack appointed Clinton as secretary of state. Barack was determined to work with former rivals, many of whom offered support to the new president.

A Long Honeymoon

Barack had scored a sweeping win in the election, garnering some 53 percent of the vote. One of the truly odd outcomes of the 2008 election, though, is that weeks after it was over, Barack still appeared to be gaining in popularity.

It is not unusual for presidents-elect to enjoy a period of popularity—a honeymoon with the American people. Americans are anxious for the new president to succeed, but many remain skeptical and some who voted for the other candidate remain bitter.

In 2000, George W. Bush won a disputed election over Vice President Al Gore—votes in Florida may have been miscounted, tilting the state to Bush, which gave the Republican the national victory. As such, when Bush prepared to take the oath of office, just 48 percent of Americans approved.

President Bill Clinton's election in 1992 was not in dispute, but when he took the oath, just 60 percent of Americans supported him. Weeks after the 2008 election, 67 percent of Americans were willing to support Barack, with most acknowledging that the problems facing the new president, and the nation, were far more serious than the problems faced by Bush and Clinton when they entered office. Said pollster Bill McInturff,

Kids listen to a reading at a book fair inside InuaguralFest in Washington, D.C. Many new books about the new president and first family have been published since Obama's election. Approval ratings for Obama and interest in his family continued to rise in the months leading up to and after the inauguration.

Obama Mania Continues

> **"Compared to Bill Clinton in '93 and Bush in '01, we're seeing a president who has been given a longer leash by the American public. This is not a traditional start of a presidency where people give you just a couple of months."**

Just before the inauguration, Barack received a remarkably high 83% approval rating for the way in which he handled the presidential transition, significantly higher than the approval level for either of his immediate predecessors just before they first took office.

Babies Named Barack

There is no question that Americans remained enthusiastic about Barack long after the votes were tallied. Some people were so ecstatic about the election that they decided to name their children after Barack. In New York, new mother Stephanie Treasure delivered her baby a day before the election, but she held off giving the boy a name until the results of the election were known. Finally, after the votes were counted, she named her son Jordan Barack Treasure. "I promised myself that if Obama became president I would name him Barack," she said. In Arizona, Decontee Williams named her new baby Barack Jeilah Williams. "I love Barack Obama and I love the name," she said.

In Africa, new mothers were even more enthusiastic. In Kenya, the country of Barack's ancestors, 23 new baby boys were named Barack while 20 new baby girls were named Michelle in the week following the election.

Some couples elected to get married and start having babies. People told reporters they had held off starting families because they didn't want to bring children into a world divided by hatred and fear. Sherry and Larry Davey of Brooklyn, New York, said they decided after the election to enlarge their family. "I feel a renewed sense of optimism and hope," said Sherry. "It does sound kind of crazy, but I really do feel hopeful."

CELEBRATING THE ELECTION

Elsewhere, people found other ways to celebrate the election of the first African-American president. In Perry County, Alabama, county commissioners voted to declare the second Monday of November Barack Obama Day, giving county employees the day off. In the election, Alabama gave McCain a majority of 60 percent, but in Perry County, whose population of about 12,000 is mostly African American, Barack won with 70 percent of the vote.

NBA star Gilbert Arenas had his own way of celebrating the victory. Shortly after the election, he had the words "Change We Believe In" (a slight variation of Barack's campaign slogan, "Change We Can Believe In") tattooed onto the fingers of his left hand. The Washington Wizards star said he got the tattoo so that during games, he could find inspiration simply by looking at his hand.

INAUGURAL BALLS

As the day of Barack's inauguration approached, the hottest tickets in the country were for places on the west side of the U.S. Capitol to attend the swearing-in ceremony. Although some 2 million people were expected to crowd into Washington, D.C., to attend the inaugural parade, balls and other events, just 240,000 tickets for the swearing-in were available.

In fact, though, there were dozens of events related to the inaugural, not only in Washington but in other cities as well. Four days before the ceremony, Barack and his family took a train ride to the capital, starting in Philadelphia and making stops in Wilmington, Delaware, and Baltimore, Maryland. The trip was intended to commemorate a similar inaugural train ride taken by Abraham Lincoln in 1861. On the day before the inaugural—Martin Luther King Jr. Day—Barack participated in a national day of community service. That night, the first ball was held—a free youth concert.

The next day, following the ceremony and the parade, dozens of parties were held around Washington. One of the most unusual

Obama Mania Continues

Spectators gathered on the National Mall in Washington, D.C., to watch as President Barack Obama takes the oath of office, January 20, 2009. About 2 million people braved the cold for hours to be a part of Obama's historic inauguration, the largest such crowd in 44 years.

OBAMA MANIA

was staged by Earl Stafford, a Virginia businessman, who spent $1 million to stage an inaugural ball for people living in poverty, people who are terminally ill, and men and women who were wounded in battle. Stafford said he was inspired by Barack's message about the importance of reaching out to others. "It's not about us but about us helping other people," Stafford said.

"Obama Eats Here"

In Chicago, tourists have started showing up at places where Barack has frequented over the years, including his barber shop as well as his favorite restaurants. One restaurant where Barack

A message board signed by more than 190,000 people from 189 countries, congratulating President Obama. One wrote, "Thank you . . . for letting me know that I can do anything!" As president, Barack Obama continues to inspire people of every color, race, and ethnic heritage throughout the world.

Obama Mania Continues

The Obama Exhibit

The election of the first African-American president in U.S. history will be commemorated by the Smithsonian Institution, the official museum of American history in Washington, D.C.

Soon after the 2008 election, the museum announced plans to stage an exhibit of Obama memorabilia at the Smithsonian's new National Museum of African American History and Culture, which is scheduled to open in 2015. The museum has taken possession of bulletin boards, tables, stacks of campaign literature, furniture (including a La-Z-Boy chair), and even trash from an Obama campaign office in Falls Church, Virginia, so that curators may recreate the scene for the museum.

has eaten many times is Medici on Chicago's South Side, where visitors can buy "Obama Eats Here" T-shirts. (The restaurant has sold more than 1,000.)

On a wall in the restaurant, visitors can also find a poem, written and tacked there by a regular customer. It reads:

> In the not so distant past
> South Chicago was cast
> As a place not particularly pleasin'.
> But from that humble place
> Began a great race
> That transformed the political season.
> On the shores of Lake Mich'
> Loomed large a grand wish
> And the cry
> Yes we can
> Yes we can.
> That cry grew quite loud
> It enraptured the crowd
> And elected our first
> Black American.

CHRONOLOGY

1961   Barack Obama is born on August 4 in Honolulu, Hawaii.

1983   Graduates from Columbia University and takes a job as a financial writer.

1984   Resigns from his corporate job and takes a job as a community organizer.

1988   Visits Kenya and enrolls at Harvard University Law School.

1989   Meets and starts dating Michelle Robinson, a young attorney who mentors him during a summer job at a Chicago law firm.

1990   Makes national headlines after being elected the first African-American president of the *Harvard Law Review*.

1991   Graduates from Harvard and works as a civil rights lawyer.

1992   Barack and Michelle marry.

1996   Wins his first political race, a seat in the Illinois State Senate.

1998   Older daughter Malia is born.

2001   Younger daughter Sasha is born.

2004   Makes "Audacity of Hope" speech to Democratic National Convention.

   Is elected to U.S. Senate representing Illinois.

2007   Kicks off candidacy for the presidency.

2008   Is elected 44th president of the United States.

2009   The Obamas move into the White House.

FUN FACTS

- Hundreds of journalists were assigned to cover Barack's inauguration; the youngest was Damon Weaver, a 10-year-old fifth-grader from K.E. Cunningham-Canal Point Elementary School in Florida. Reporting for his school's TV station, Weaver had already snagged interviews with Vice President-elect Joe Biden, Caroline Kennedy, and NBA player Dwayne Wade when the inaugural committee agreed to admit him to the events in Washington.

- The crowd of 2 million or more who attended Barack's inaugural festivities was the largest in 44 years; the previous record was set in 1965 by the 1.2 million people who attended the inaugural of President Lyndon B. Johnson.

- When Barack was a teenager he was a devoted fan of Spider-Man; in January 2009, Barack finally got to meet his hero, albeit on the pages of a Spider-Man comic book. Marvel Comics, the publisher, featured the new president in an episode in which Spider-Man thwarts a plan by Chameleon to disrupt the inaugural events.

- Michelle has also been featured in a comic book—she is the main character in a series titled "Female Force" in which the stories of famous women are dramatized.

- Chocolate chunk cookies from Baby Boomers Café in Des Moines, Iowa, have become a national sensation. The reason: Sasha and Malia became big fans of the cookies when they visited their father's campaign headquarters in the weeks leading up to the Iowa caucuses.

- One of the newest tourist hot spots in Chicago is Coye's Barber Shop, which is where Barack got his hair cut before his election as president. Since the election, Coye's owner reports about five tourists a day, many of them Europeans, ask to get their hair cut at the shop.

- After the 2008 election, an online bookseller said buyers have been paying as much as $5,500 for signed copies of Barack's 1995 memoir, *Dreams from My Father*.

- Within 24 hours of Barack's victory, the news Web site CNN.com sold 5,000 T-shirts emblazoned with CNN's headline "Obama Inspires Historic Victory" as well as the time and date the headline appeared on network, 11:04 p.m. November 4, 2008.

- HBO started work on a documentary about Barack in 2006; the finished film is expected to air on the network in 2009 or 2010.

- Barack's decision to seek votes from young people paid off. Statistics showed he captured 66 percent of the vote of people between the ages of 18 and 29; in 2008, about 24 million Americans in that age group cast ballots, about 2 million more than in 2004.

GLOSSARY

anchors—On television news broadcasts, journalists who read news items and introduce stories produced by field reporters.

autobiography—Book written by a person, often someone who has achieved fame, who tells the story of his or her background and the deeds that led to their renown.

blog—Short for web log.

cabinet—Panel composed of the president's major advisers who, in turn, head departments of the federal government.

caucuses—Events used by some states to award delegates to presidential candidates; in a caucus, voters meet in groups and cast their ballots in public.

civil rights—Rights defined by the U.S. Constitution that guarantee all Americans equal treatment under law, such as the right to vote.

columnist—Newspaper or magazine journalist who offers opinions on issues.

foreign policy—The official position taken by one country in its relationships with other countries.

intern—Student who works in a professional position while going to school; the job is intended to give the student hands-on experience.

journalists—Professionals who report and write the news that is featured in newspapers, magazines, TV and radio broadcasts, and Internet-based news sources.

keynote address—The major speech delivered at the opening of the national political conventions, or similar events, intended to set the tone for the conventions.

mentor—To act as a trusted counselor or guide.

Middle East—Region of southwest Asia and northern Africa marked by turmoil, often prompted by religious differences among its people.

primary—Process used by many states to select nominees for fall elections and award delegates to presidential candidates; in a typical primary, the voter casts a ballot in secret in a voting booth. Delegates are elected to support presidential candidates based on the number of popular votes they receive.

scholarship—Financial assistance offered by a school or college to help a student pay the cost of tuition.

FURTHER READING & INTERNET RESOURCES

Books and Periodicals

Booth, William. "Obama's On-the-Wall Endorsement," *Washington Post* (May 18, 2008)

Obama, Barack. *The Audacity of Hope: Thoughts on Reclaiming the American Dream.* New York: Three Rivers Press, 2006.

———. *Dreams from My Father: A Story of Race and Inheritance*. New York: Crown, 2004.

Pilkington, Ed. "U.S. Election: He Could Read a Directory and it Would Sound Good," *The Guardian* (August 27, 2008)

Editors of *Slate*. *Obamamania!: The English Language, Barackafied*. New York: Fireside, 2008.

Rabinowitz, Michelle. "New Hampshire '08: A Day in the Life of a Barack Obama Volunteer," MTV News, January 11, 2008, www.mtv.com/news/articles/1579488/20080111/index.jhtml.

Small, Jay-Newton. "Obama's Celebrity Army," *Time* (February 4, 2008)

Sullivan, Robert, editor. *The American Journey of Barack Obama: From Boyhood to the White House.* New York: Little, Brown and Company, 2008.

Web Sites

www.barackobama.com

Obama for America, the campaign committee that worked to elect Barack Obama to the presidency, maintains a Web site that explains the issues the 44th president must tackle during his administration. Students can find biographies of Barack and Michelle and read copies of some of Barack's major speeches.

www.pic2009.org

The Web site maintained by the Presidential Inaugural Committee highlights the dozens of events planned around Barack's inauguration in early 2009.

www.obamain30seconds.org

The political activist group Moveon.org sponsored a contest for amateur filmmakers to produce their own 30-second campaign commercials for Barack. More than 1,100 responded. The winners of the competition as well as many others are posted on the contest Web site.

www.jfklibrary.org

Barack has often been compared to the 35th president, John F. Kennedy. Visitors to the Web site maintained by the late president's library can read about his administration, read profiles of the president and members of his family, and search through entries in the president's diary for significant events in history.

INDEX

Affleck, Ben, 32
African Americans, and Obama's election, 11, 15
Aniston, Jennifer, 44
Arenas, Gilbert, 54
Armisen, Fred, 47
Audacity of Hope, The (book), 28
"Audacity of Hope, The" (speech), 25–28
Avila, Ross, 15

Barack Obama Day, 54
Barack O'Lanterns, 42
basketball, 21–22, 33, 38
Becchi, Theresa, 26–27
Behar, Joy, 35
Berlin, 37–41
Berry, Halle, 45
Biden, Joe, 45
Black Eyed Peas, 33–34
Broder, David, 38
Brown, Gordon, 49
Bush, George W., 38, 41, 47, 51–52

cabinet, 50
campaigning, 21–23, 29–33, 37–42
Cannon, Nick, 35
celebrity endorsements, 42–45
civil rights movement, 15, 27, 39
Clinton, Bill, 52
Clinton, Hillary Rodham, 13, 37, 47, 50
Clooney, George, 45
Collymore, Karol, 27
Craig, Jim, 28
Cummings, Elijah, 12
Cyrus, Miley, 32

Damon, Matt, 32
Davey, Larry and Sherry, 53
Democratic National Convention, 25–28
DeNiro, Robert, 45
Dreams from My Father (book), 18–20
Dunham, Stanley Ann, 20–21

eBay, 47
election, celebrations of, 11, 15, 49, 54, 57
Ellen DeGeneres Show, The (TV show), 33
Ettinger, Amber Lee, 32

Fairey, Shepard, 35, 42
Ferrell, Will, 47
Fey, Tina, 47
fist bump, 35
Flickr, 32
foreign policy, 38
fundraising, 32–33

Germany, 37–41
Goldberg, Whoopi, 35
Gore, Al, 51
Grant Park celebration, 11, 15, 49

Hanks, Tom, 45
Harvard Law Review, 17, 23
Harvard University Law School, 17, 21
Hasselbeck, Elisabeth, 35
Hemmer, Bill, 28
Hill, E. D., 35
honeymoon, presidential, 51–53
Hu, Kelly, 34

inauguration, celebrations of, 54–56
Internet
    and campaign, 13, 32–33, 42
    and Obama stuff, 47
Iraq War, 30–31, 38, 50

Jackson, Jesse, 15
Jackson, Samuel L., 45
Johansson, Scarlett, 34, 45

Kennedy, Caroline, 12
Kennedy, Edward M., 12
Kennedy, John F., 12
Kenya, 18, 20, 53

INDEX

keynote address, 25–28
Khubani, A. J., 47
King, Martin Luther, Jr., 39–41
Krause, Manfred, 39–41

Late Show with David Letterman (TV show), 33
Legend, John, 35
Lowery, Joseph, 27

Maurer, Suzanne, 21
McCain, John, 11, 41, 47, 50, 54
McInturff, Bill, 52–53
Meyer, Cordula, 41
Middle East, 38
Motlanthe, Kgalema, 50
Moveon.org, 32
multiracial persons, 17–21
MySpace, 32, 45

National Museum of African American History and Culture, 49, 54, 57
Ndobe, Kim, 31
Norton, Ed, 44

Obama, Barack, 17–23
   popularity of, 11–15, 25–37, 49–57
   as speaker, 25–28, 30
Obama, Barack, Sr., 20
Obama, Malia Ann, 15, 21
Obama, Michelle Robinson, 15, 21–22, 27, 35, 53
Obama, Sasha (Natasha), 15, 21
"Obama Girl," 32
"Obama in 30 Seconds" contest, 32
Obama mania, 11–15, 49–57
   beginning of, 25–35
Obama stuff, 37–45
Owens, John, 18

Palin, Sarah, 47
Palmor, Ygal, 50

Poehler, Amy, 47
posters, 35, 42

race relations, Obama on, 18–20
Robinson, Craig, 22
Rock, Chris, 44–45
Rodriguez, John, 35

Sarkozy, Nicholas, 49
Saturday Night Live (TV show), 33, 47
Schulz, Gerda, 41
Schwarzenegger, Arnold, 12
Shepherd, Sherri, 35
Shriver, Maria, 12
Smithsonian Institution, 57
Soetoro-Ng, Maya, 21
Stafford, Earl, 56
Stuttaford, Andrew, 42

text messaging, 45
Treasure, Jordan Barack, 53

Valetta, Amber, 35
View, The (TV show), 35

Walsh, Kate, 34
Walters, Barbara, 35
Werksman, Ruth, 27
Widmer, Ted, 30
will.i.am, 33–34
Williams, Barack Jeila, 53
Winfrey, Oprah, 15, 43–44
Woodward, Alfre, 44

"Yes, we can" slogan, 39, 47
"Yes We Can" (song), 30
young people, and Obama's campaign, 13–15, 30–31
YouTube, 32, 35

PICTURE CREDITS

page

- **2:** Alan Chen/IOA; Erard Swannet/IOA; Aaron Edwards/IOA; Itsuo Inouye/AP Photo; mayhem/IOA Photos; Obama for America/PRMS; Obama for America/PRMS; Charles Rex Arbogast/AP Photo; Obama for America/PRMS; Paul McRae/IOA
- **7:** Bill Greenblatt/UPI Photo
- **10:** Josh Copeland/IOA; Young Yun/IOA; Pete Prodoehl/IOA; Charlie Nguyen/IOA
- **13:** Obama for America/NMI
- **14:** New Millennium Images
- **16:** Obama for America/PRMS
- **19:** Nathan F./IOA Photos
- **20:** Obama for America/PRMS
- **23:** Mark Pokempner/CIC
- **24:** Daniel Bersak/Sipa Press
- **26:** Peter Howe/IOA Photos
- **29:** Lydia T. Wagner/IOA Photos
- **31:** Sarah Kennon/IOA Photos
- **33:** Steve Jurvetson/IOA Photos
- **34:** Steve Rhodes/IOA Photos
- **36:** Obama for America/PRMS; TheGirlsNY/IOA; Adam Berry/Bloomberg News; Sugar Pond/IOA
- **39:** .Kai/IOW Photos
- **40:** nagaremono/IOW; julieb1975/IOW; Steve Chasmar/IOW; Rajeev Gupta/IOW
- **43:** Shasti O'Leary Soudant/IOA Photos
- **44:** Obama for America/PRMS
- **46:** Amy B./IOA; Art by Mags/IOA; Jennoit/IOA; Steve Rhodes/IOA
- **48:** Marisa Arrona/IOA Photos
- **51:** Washington Times/MCT
- **52:** onourminds/IOA Photos
- **55:** Brett Familoe/IOA Photos
- **56:** Robin Presta/IOA Photos

Front cover: (from top left) Alan Chen/IOA; Erard Swannet/IOA; Aaron Edwards/IOA; Itsuo Inouye/AP Photo; mayhem/IOA Photos; Obama for America/PRMS; Obama for America/PRMS; Charles Rex Arbogast/AP Photo; Obama for America/PRMS; Paul McRae/IOA

ABOUT THE AUTHOR

Hal Marcovitz is a former newspaper reporter who has written more than 100 books for young readers. In 2005, *Nancy Pelosi*, his biography of House Speaker Nancy Pelosi, was named to *Booklist* magazine's list of recommended feminist books for young readers. He lives in Chalfont, Pennsylvania, with his wife Gail and daughter Ashley.